FROM SLAVERY TO SONSHIP

C. G. MYLREA

From Slavery to Sonship

THE MASS MOVEMENTS AMONG THE OUTCASTES OF INDIA

At different periods in the history of the world great movements come to the birth, fraught with far-reaching consequences to the spiritual progress of mankind. Some within and some without the Church, they serve to inspire the men of vision and faith, and to prove afresh that the government of God is sleeplessly active in the control of the destinies of man.

Of such a character are the mass movements among the outcastes of India. For nearly a century these have been spreading over the whole land and gathering force with every decade, until at the present moment they are outstanding features of missions in India.

Contents

Foreword

Published by:
TINNEVELLY CHRISTIAN HISTORICAL SOCIETY
2.2.3(4), North Street,
Bungalow Surandai-627859
Tenkasi district (Tirunelveli)
04633-290401, +91 91767 80001,+91 75388 12218
https://christianhistoricalsociety.in
https://tchsportal.co.in/
Email : christianhistorical@gmail.com

From Slavery to Sonship
in English
By C. G. MYLREA

Printed at : TCHS Press

Enter Caption

CHAPTER ONE

THE MASS MOVEMENTS AMONG THE OUTCASTES OF INDIA

From Slavery to Sonship

At different periods in the history of the world great movements come to the birth, fraught with far-reaching consequences to the spiritual progress of mankind. Some within and some without the Church, they serve to inspire the men of vision and faith, and to prove afresh that the government of God is sleeplessly active in the control of the destinies of man.

Of such a character are the mass movements among the outcastes of India. For nearly a century these have been spreading over the whole land and gathering force with every decade, until at the present moment they are outstanding features of missions in India.

The Right Rev. V. S. Azariah, of Dornakal,
The First Indian Bishop

Working on lines of his own he is developing a most promising Church among the depressed classes

Vast Numbers

The Unique Opportunity The opportunity is absolutely unparalleled in the history of Christendom. Never before have such large communities of idolaters been drawn towards the Christian faith, and never before have the resultant problems been of greater importance to the Church at large. The movement is unique both for the number of people and the vastness of the area affected, and also for its peculiar relation to the social conditions of India.

The number of outcastes is estimated to be between fifty and sixty millions, or one-sixth of the total population, and the extent to which the whole body of these peoples has already been affected by the Gospel may be gathered from the fact that nearly half a million of them have been enrolled in the Christian Church through the instrumentality of all the Protestant bodies during the last five years.

Wide Area of the Movements

Then these outcaste communities are found in every part of India, from Travancore to the Himalayas While they are alike in their religious degradation and their menial position as the field laborers of India, they are divided from one another by every variety of language, race, and climate. Yet all through this diversity a movement, one in its characteristics, has been gathering force for the last half century. This vast, inanimate mass has seemed to feel a new pulsing of life, and has begun to move towards the light, breaking away from the old customs and making for the unknown land of a new faith. Not in units, not even only in families, but often as a whole clan they accept Christian teaching at the same time, and enter together by baptism into the Christian Church. It is this condition which is connoted by the term "Mass Movement."

Thousands have thus been added to the visible Church within the last few years, who have not yet had time to develop into mature and solid Christians: thousands more are in the stage of being taught the simple elements of the Christian Faith; while multitudes are without, willing, and in some cases eager, to learn but compelled by the absence of workers to ask for instruction in vain.

The facts must be widely known if the interest and conscience of the Church are to be quickened; friends of missions must understand what this movement is, and why an appeal goes forth now, at this crisis in our national history. The opportunity will not wait; the very success of work among Outcastes makes an appeal inevitable. Retreat is out of the question; advance is alike the highest Christian strategy and the only way of victory.

Social Degradation

The social condition of the Outcastes is at once the condemnation of the "caste" system and a challenge to the "free" peoples of the West to come to their aid. Its chief characteristics are the stigma of a debased spiritual state, a position of virtual slavery, dense ignorance, and hopeless poverty.

In varying degrees in North and South India the Outcaste is unclean to the Hindu; he is the "untouchable" one, and in Travancore even unapproachable." Under the inexorable law that a man's status is absolutely and irrevocably fixed by birth, the lot of these unfortunate people has become a prison from which no escape is possible. In the towns he is the sweeper, the scavenger, the menial servant, but in the villages--and it must be remembered that over ninety per cent of the population of India live in villages-he is the farm laborer, the serf of the landlords and wealthy tenants, bearing the burden of the hardest tasks under a tropical sun. He lives in a mud cottage, and even this is not his own properly: his rights are almost non-existent, and though the most necessary element to the economic system he is the least considered.

The Coming Change

But a change is coming, rather has come, with portentous bearings on the future both of Hinduism and Christianity. The prisoner has felt the bars of his cage and is making a bid for freedom. The conviction that in Christ alone is their hope is gradually permeating these depressed classes, and the desire to raise both socially and spiritually is finding expression in an insistent hammering at the doors of the Christian Church. The chains are not broken at once, even though the prison doors are open; the heredity of a thousand years is not dispelled in a generation; the way towards a free and sturdy faith is long and difficult; but the Outcaste is awake, he has found that there is a more human and generous faith than Hinduism. and is moving out of ignorance and bondage into the glorious liberty of the children of God.

The Baptism of Forty - five Outcastes in the Telugu Country

CHAPTER TWO

A Church in the Making

A few pictures drawn from the field will illustrate how this is coming to pass, and for this purpose the field of the United Provinces of Agra and Oudh has been chosen as affording typical scenes of village work.

This part of the Gangetic plain is a tract of country densely covered with villages, intersected with great rivers and canals, but not too well supplied with metalled roads. The Outcastes are found in large clans between the Ganges and the Jumna, more than a million living in the C.M.S. districts alone. While not everywhere equally ready to accept baptism, they are almost universally willing to become inquirers. And this in itself constitutes a most unusual opportunity.

Gathering Momentum

But it is the gathering momentum of the movement which is most impressive. Some years **ago there was it is true an**

incipient desire, yet withal suspicion and half-heartedness. Later came a period of isolated invitations, with a crop of failures and some lapses. At the present time the missionaries are beset with insistent appeals, to have to decline which continually is enough to break an earnest worker's heart. For example: during the camping of 1916-17, after a baptism of 124 souls at Bopara in the Meerut district, Mr. Perfumi had deputations from four Chamar (leatherworker) villages for teachers: at another baptism at Anti, about twenty miles away, requests came from five villages yet me visited. Of yet another village asking for baptism Mi. Perfumi writes, " Their earnestness is very great."

The dominant motive is no doubt the desire for social uplift; but when this is met, not with merely secular teaching but with the Gospel of Christ, the poor oppressed toilers soon learn that true liberty can only be found in the Lord Jesus Christ, and the whole movement is thus spiritualized.

Stages of Growth

There are stages in the growth of these Churches, as in the human being--infancy, adolescence, and maturity. To the last stage possibly no Church from the Outcastes has yet attained in any part of India: some however are in the position of adolescence, but in the United Provinces none have yet emerged from infancy.

Infancy.

The first stage is pre-eminently that of the teacher, for the time of the pastors has not yet come. Let us watch the former at work.

Typical Scenes

The Chamar or the sweeper is nearly always at Work all day, so the evening is often the only time to get the men together, Word has been sent to a village and at sunset the party of teachers arrives. One by one the Christians and inquirers gather outside their huts under a mango tree, all sitting on a red cloth reserved for this use, the missionary possibly sitting too on the ground or a low stool. In the deepening twilight the service is held; Christian hymus are sung, and short prayers are offered, the Lord's Prayer being repeated by nearly all present. Then follows a brief catechizing to test how far the inquirers have made progress and whether they are fit for baptism; after the service friendly chat drives home what has been taught. Or it may be late at night when a distant village is reached; news has been sent ahead and the party is met at the village entry by some of the head men. By the dim light of an oil lantern they pick their way through the narrow and dirty alleys till they come to the mud platform where the congregation is waiting. It is a true Rembrandt picture-the fitful rays of the lantern falling on the dusky figures of the boys in front, and the serried rows of men behind them, while the women stealthily Creep up and remain lurking in the shadows. Some of the answers show that Christian truth is sinking down into these untaught minds, while again others find great difficulty in acquiring even the most elementary facts.

Persecution

Yet they must be tested, and where perhaps the missionary fails, the Hindu caste man comes in. There is seldom absence of persecution, and often the most grievous hostility is shown by the landlords towards their quasi-serfs. Personal violence, unjust lawsuits, deprivation of grazing rights, arson, eviction, are some of the methods employed, and yet the inquirers often show a noble courage. The steel so tested will not fail in the hour of stress and battle.

Then comes the great day of confession, when the rubicon is finally crossed, when in Christian baptism they sever themselves from their old life, and enter into the fellowship of the Body of Christ. Thus are formed the little groups of Christians in the scattered villages of the plains of India, tiny points of light now, but destined under God to be light bearers to their fellow-countrymen and channels of blessing to their persecutors.

The day of their baptism is not only a red-letter day for the new converts, but also furnishes an object lesson to all castes and classes living in the villages nearby. It is, moreover, frequently the means of bringing waverers to the point, and inducing the more timid to become regular inquirers. Stories might be indefinitely multiplied to illustrate this, but the following has a peculiar pathos.

While the missionaries were camped in the Meerui district, giving final instruction before a baptism, day by day deputations came in from surrounding villages to ask for teachers. Among these came a woman with her two children, asking for immediate baptism. As she had not been taught. This could not be granted. After much importunity, in despair she offered her children to be taken to Meerut and brought up as Christians, and seemed to be satisfied when this was gladly acceded to. However as the baptismal service proceeded, at which fifty-four were admitted, she songht, but in vain, to be baptized by taking her place with the women, but had to be gently refused. As the camp broke up. When her children had gone, she came for a final word with Mr. Perfumi. "Will you soon baptize my children?" "Yes, that is why I have taken them." Then, with tears, “And if in the coming months I should die in my outcaste state, will my children deny me before the great Lord?”

When she, too, has learned the faith more fully, may she not prove a real light of her village and the witness of a faith which will bind all in one here and hereafter?

Adolescence. *- But the period of adolescence sooll begins and with this the whole problem of schools primary schools for the village children, boarding schools for the brighter boys and girls who will make the future teachers, and lastly training schools where teachers and pastors may be prepared for their work.*

The Crucial Factor

The point to be grasped is that the evangelizing of these millions of Outcastes depends on the Creation of the indigenous worker; without an army of teachers, preachers, and pastors drawn from the peoples themselves, the task must remain beyond fulfillment. In every field this is admitted, and it has also been recognized that a beginning must be made at the very bottom. The key of the whole question is the village school. Every community, as soon as it has been established, should be provided with a school, however elementary. This ideal has hitherto not been reached owing to the dearth of teachers and of the means of paying them: even in the Telugu Mission, the most advanced field, out of 850 congregations only 345 have schools, while in the United Provinces only a very small proportion of the villages have resident teachers.

Economic Difficulties

The problem is complicated by the labour aspect of **the question. Where every member of** the family after the tenderest years is a wage earner and every handful of grain brought in means the relief of actual hunger, it is difficult for the parents to realize that the future of the Faith rests on these children going to school, and the temptation to keep them at home is very strong indeed.

Need of Pure Environment

But while this is the first, it is only the first rung **of the ladder. The sharpest and most in** tell gent children must be passed on to the district boarding schools. Here in a Christian armosphere they can develop in body, mind. And spirit until they get their certificates as teachers and can go out to man the village schools. If any show marked ability, the central high school can take them and enable them to go on, with ordination as their goal, to be leaders in their own Church

The process is long, and the best results will not appear in the first, or even perhaps in the second generation; it also involves considerable outlay both for buildings and staff. But there is no short cut. It is here we must be prepared to help, at once and substantially. The process is vital and strategic and at the same time practical and remunerative.

Visible Fruit

The older missions in the South have this machinery at work, and the children of the boarding schools are the great hope of the Church, No one who has seen these young people in their orderly worship, with their bright, intelligent faces and clean clothes, and contrasted them with their pre-Christian state, but must own that they constitute a very miracle of grace.

Maturity. ***This stage has yet to be attained, but the ideal is ever before the eyes of the missionary force; it is that of a robust and vigorous indigenous Church, combining in it the functions of self-support, self-government, and self-extension.***

Every plan, ovary reinforcement, every appeal must have this end in view, both as a pledge to those who give and pray at home, as a token of sincerity to the Indians themselves, and as a means of truly extending the Church of God in the world.

Outcaste Boys Learning in a Village School

CHAPTER THREE

The C.M.S. Missions

Travancore

Earliest of all Missions to realize the claim of the Outcaste to the Gospel was the Church Missionary Society working in the State of Travancore. As far back as 1821 the first converts were baptized, but the movement did not really get a firm hold till thirty years later. Then progress was rapid, and 5000 were brought in between 1850 and 1860. Since that time there has been no looking back, and though at times the annual addition of a thousand converts has not always been maintained, there has been steady growth, and out of the 60,000 Anglicans in North Travancore today, about 40,000 have been won from these untouchables. There is a well-developed system of native Church councils, and the people themselves out of their poverty contribute generously towards the maintenance of their pastors.

Yet the Home Church has only half-heartedly done her duty by this Mission. The boarding schools live from hand to mouth, and the training institutions are with difficulty financed. It is in these directions especially that the Mission needs home support: if this is withheld its growth must be stunted and its life wanting in power.

2. Telugu Country

The Telugu field was occupied in 1841, mainly as the result of appeals from laymen in the service **of the East India Company, but** for more than twenty years the continuity of missionaries in this work was constantly broken. In nearly every case the beginnings were small, and there was little else than the faith of devoted men to prove that the movement among the Outcastes would become widespread and fruitful. Not till the decade 1860-70 did converts come in numbers, but since then continuous progress has been maintained. And of late years the growth has been in some instances remarkably rapid. This Mission is fortunate in having the first Indian bishop, Bishop Azariah of Dornakal. In its midst. Working on lines of his own he is developing a most promising Church among the depressed classes.

All the five districts of the Teluga Mission show encouraging results, as their statistics indicate. In 1900 there were 482 village congregations with 13,141 baptized Christians; in 1918 there were over 3000 such congregations with a roll of 32,737 Christians. In the same period the number of inquirers had risen from 3289 to 10.718; the number of schools was doubled; and the contributions from the Churches had risen from Rs 4364 in 1895 to Rs 21.762.

These figures show that the work is expanding. Increasing in fact faster than the resources of the Mission will allow. The need for subdividing the large districts and for more Indian workers is acute. As in the case of Travancore it is the boarding schools which must at all costs be enlarged. This statement is borne out by a quotation from Canon Sell's report for 1913

In these growing districts the importance of efficient boarding schools is great. They form the basis of all plans for dealing with mass movements. The reason is plain. The human agency for such work is the village schoolmaster or schoolmistress. These workers come from training institutions, but whence are their students obtained ? From the boarding schools and from the boarding schools alone. If then these languish for want of funds to maintain boys and girls for a few years, the whole machinery of the Mission collapses.... This then is the reason why we so earnestly appeal for this form of help. An impoverished boarding school means that some years hence the work of the past may be ruined, and what once bid fair to become a garden of the Lord may relapse into a dreary wilderness.

3. The Punjab

The next large Mission to be affected by the mass movement among the Outcastes was the Punjab. Here as in other parts of North India the earlier efforts of the missionaries were directed to winning the higher castes, and it is only within the last twenty-five years that the Chuhras, as the great outcaste clan in the Punjab is called, have begun to be gathered in. The movement among these communities has been very rapid and the C.M.S. Mission has taken its share, with the result that some 25,000 have become members of our Church. The Chuhra is of a higher type than most of the Outcastes in South India, and at least two converts have risen to be pastors and preachers of the first rank.

The outstanding need of this Mission is the subdivision of the huge districts now utterly beyond the power of the staff, with the provision which this will entail of more

Indian and European leaders to superintend the districts efficiently.

4. The United Provinces

Not till ten years ago did the districts of Meerut and Aligarh begin to gather in a harvest **of souls, though for many years before** this there had been desultory work among the sweepers. The last four year's however have seen such a marked advance that a special appeal has been deemed essential both for reinforcements and funds. The staff is utterly inadequate to deal with the new Converts or the growing numbers of inquirers and only by special help is it possible to deal with the situation. The machinery in this Mission for the training of village workers is only in its embryonic stages, and the need of Christian boarding schools is just beginning to be felt; but with half as many inquirers as there are baptized members of the Church, and an equally large number of would-be inquirers not yet under instruction, there is no doubt that immediate steps must be taken to strengthen the Mission.

5. Western India

In addition, the latest reports from the Western India Mission show that for some little time there has been a mass movement inprogress around Aurangabad; many village congregations have been enrolled and a few schools opened, but this part of the Mission has had no chance to develop. Invitations from many villages have been declined from lack of workers, and the number of resident teachers is woefully inadequate. With a view to calling attention to a most promising field, the Mission has followed the example of the United Provinces and has sent home a detailed survey and appeal.

Although God has given us this unique and unparalleled opportunity, up to the present neither has Christian strategy fully perceived it, nor have Christian service and liberality enabled us to take advantage of it. A little interest in a particular field here and there has from time to time been aroused, and a few offers of service secured, but the magnitude of the task of gathering in a strong and living Church from the Outcastes all over India has yet to capture the imagination of the Christian world.

A Contrast
Two Families of Outcastes - that on the left Heathen, that on the right Christian

CHAPTER FOUR

The Urgency of the Need

The work has been begun and has been blessed out of all proportion to the human agency Summary employed, but the situation now in every field may be summed up in a few words. There are everywhere more Christians than can be shepherded, more children than can be taught, more inquirers than can be instructed; and there are hundreds of invitations from the heathen to send teachers that have to be refused.

The need is for thorough reinforcement, both in workers and funds.

European Staff

In every area the missionaries are working to breaking point and there are no reserves. At the close of 1916 a missionary in Travancore passed to his rest, one who was heart and soul devoted to this work, and there is no one to take his place. Were a similar thing to occur in any other mass movement area, the same predicament would result.

The very fact that the world war has called forth sacrifice on a scale never before equalled in the history of the world encourages the hope perceived, the appeal of the Cross will prove as irresistible as it has ever done in the past.

Indian Workers

Every effort is being made to call out the reserves of India's sons and daughters. but as has been shown, all depends on our establishing sufficient schools of all classes, stalling them efficiently, and filling them with students.

The Call of the Present

The reasons for putting out such an appeal in this e time of national strain lie in the danger of further delay. Not only may the opportunity pass away, but the harm which inaction is doing may soon prove irreparable. There are two main facts which are full of danger to these immature Christian communities; one is the imperfect apprehension of the Truth, and the other is the illiterate state of the mass of the people. The first tends largely to vitiate the power of Christian witness, and the other stands in the way of the progress of the Church to a higher level.

A further consideration is the activity of non Christian bodies who, moved with jealousy at the success of missionary efforts, are leaving no stone unturned to retain the Outcastes within the pale of Hinduism. Yet another reason will have weight with many. The Anglican heritage is rich in this part of the great vineyard, but if we are now deaf to this appeal, thousands will be gathered in by other Christian bodies, and a source of spiritual wealth and grace to our Church be lost to her forever.

The present condition of poverty militates against self-support in the early stages, but there is no reason for the suspicion that water is poured into a sieve. With instruction in the Christian faith, and elementary education, the communities will rise in the moral and social scale, the material resources of the Church will improve, and thus in due time the question will solve itself.

The Appeal

Can we help? The challenge to faith is clear. To deny the ability to respond is to confess spiritual bankruptcy, and to admit that after all material issues are the only ones that count.

There is only one answer possible to us, if we believe that the Great Commission is still binding. GOD IS READY, and has shown this clearly in the way in which these millions, crushed for centuries under the iron heel of caste, are now willing and eager to be taught and baptized-God is ready, even in this time of straightness, to prove that He is equal to all emergencies, and that this our extremity is His opportunity. But the essential conditions must be present faith in God, and surrender to Him of lives and wills. Of talents and means.

THIS IS OUR PART. Wherever man has so proved God. He has never failed. The issue narrows down to the individual, the reader into whose hands this booklet may fall. Let our Christian heritage, our devotion to a common faith, our sympathy with the backward and oppressed ones of the earth, alike impel us to look up to our expectant Lord and say. "Here am 1: send me."

C. G. MYLREA

CHURCH MISSTOKARY SOCIETY, SALISBURY SQUARE, E.C. 4.

Printed by Libri Plureos GmbH in Hamburg, Germany